This Walker book belongs to:

Scarlett Olivia

Roberge

★ *For Lily John, who showed me her fairy letters,*
and for Josie, just because ★ *A.D.*

★ *For Helena, Denise and Julie,*
thank you all ★ *V.C.*

First published 2003 by Walker Books Ltd
87 Vauxhall Walk, London SE11 5HJ
This edition published 2014

10 9 8 7 6

Text © 2003, 2014 Alan Durant
Illustrations © 2003 Vanessa Cabban

British Library Cataloguing in Publication Data:
a catalogue record for this book is available from the British Library

ISBN 978-1-4063-5336-5

www.walker.co.uk

WALKER BOOKS
AND SUBSIDIARIES
LONDON · BOSTON · SYDNEY · AUCKLAND

Dear Tooth Fairy

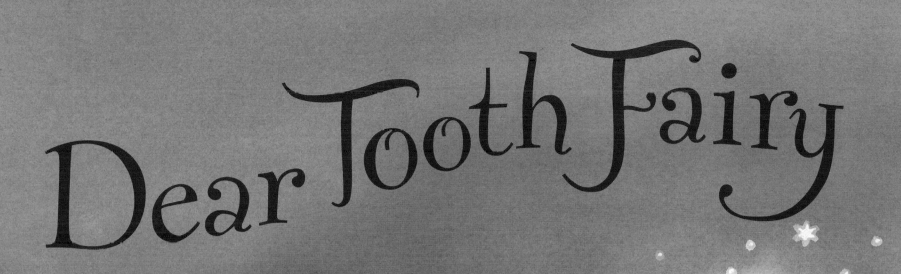

Alan Durant

illustrated by

Vanessa Cabban

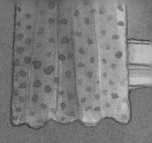

olly's tooth was wobbly. It got wobblier
and wobblier … and then it fell out!
I could give it to the Tooth Fairy, she thought,
and get a coin. But Holly liked her tooth
and wanted to keep it. So she put some plastic
vampire fangs under her pillow instead.

"The Tooth Fairy should be happy, because
she's getting *lots* of teeth," she said to herself.
Next morning the vampire fangs were still there.
But there was a tiny letter too.

WE NEED YOUR TEETH

Holly read the note from the Tooth Fairy
over and over. She was so pleased.
I must write back, she thought. This
is what she wrote:

Dear Tooth Fairy,
Thank you for coming last night! I've
never had a visit from a tooth fairy before.
Could you answer some questions please?
What do you want my tooth for?
How did you know it had come out?
Are there Lots of tooth fairies or
are you the only one?
Where do you live?
Please answer.
Love Holly

P.S. I drew a picture of you.
I hope you like it.

Holly put the letter
under her pillow.

That night the Tooth Fairy came back.

When Holly looked under her pillow
next morning, her note had gone.
In its place was a new letter.

Holly read the letter. She thought
about all the tooth fairies, flying hither
and thither through the starry sky.

No 2 Tooth House
Flower Lane Fairyland

Dear Holly,

Questions, questions!
We tooth fairies are very busy, you know.
Luckily there are lots of us. Each night, we fly
hither and thither around the world from our
home in Fairyland, collecting teeth. Human
teeth are very useful to fairies. They are white
(our favourite colour), strong and last a long
time. At the moment we are using the teeth
to build a palace for the Fairy Queen. I knew
your tooth had fallen out because the tips of
my wings tingled. In fact they tingled a lot,
which means yours is a very good tooth. You
must have been looking after it very well!
I look forward to seeing it tonight when
I return. Please leave it under your pillow!

The Tooth Fairy

PS Your drawing was very good
– only a little too green!

All that day Holly wondered about Fairyland and what it must be like. She wrote another note to the Tooth Fairy.

Dear Tooth Fairy,
Thank you so much for your letter.
I'm glad you liked my picture, but
(please don't be cross!!!) there's
just one more thing I need to know
(well, two things actually).
Are there lots of different sorts of fairy?
And what do they do all day and night?
If the fairies want my tooth, I need to know
that they will be good owners, don't I?

Love,
Holly

That night the Tooth Fairy
visited once more.

No 2 Tooth House   Flower Lane   Fairyland

Dear Holly,

I'll tell you what this fairy does all day and night: waits around for
you to give her your tooth! However, as I really need your tooth for the
Fairy Queen's palace, I shall answer these questions. But NO MORE!
This leaflet shows some of the different kinds of fairy and what they do.
Most fairies are very useful – except boggarts, who are a nuisance!
Now, please will you let me have that tooth!

The Tooth Fairy

Meet the
FAIRIES

Holly read the letter and studied her leaflet. She liked it very much. She wanted to help the Tooth Fairy but she still wasn't sure about giving up her tooth. Then she had an idea.

Dear Tooth Fairy,
Thank you for the leaflet! It's beautiful!
   I think all the fairies are lovely, but I like tooth fairies the best!
   Do you like riddles? I do! Here's a challenge for you. If you ask me a riddle that I can't answer then I'll give you my tooth.
   That's fair isn't it? By the way, I think I know one of those boggarts— my little brother!
                                    Love Holly

That night, for the fourth time,
the Tooth Fairy came.

No 2 Tooth House
Flower Lane Fairyland

Dear Holly,

How clever you are – I think you might make
a good fairy. We fairies love riddles! I've left
you a little fairy riddle book with this letter.
I hope you'll enjoy sharing it with your friends!
Now, here is your challenge:

Riddle-me-roo, riddle-me-ree
Why is a tooth like a tree?

The Fairy Queen's palace is finished, except
for one thing: her throne. Only the best tooth
will do for this and that is why I need your
tooth so badly. But if I do not receive it tonight,
I shall not bother you again. If you really want
to keep it, I would not want to take it from you.

Best wishes
The Tooth Fairy

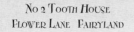

FAIRY
RIDDLE
BOOK

Holly loved her fairy riddle book. It was the best present she'd ever had. She knew that it was now time to give the Tooth Fairy a present in return. That evening Holly put her tooth under her pillow.

"Goodbye, tooth," she said, and she left a final note for the Tooth Fairy.

Dear Tooth Fairy,
The answer to your riddle is they both have roots. But don't worry, I'm giving you my tooth anyway, because I know how much you need it.
I hope the Fairy Queen likes her new throne.
Thank you very much for visiting me and being so patient.
I hope I hear from you again some time.
Goodbye!
Lots of love, Holly ×××

That night, for the last time,
the Tooth Fairy came.
She took Holly's tooth and left
a letter. Then she flew away back
to Fairyland.

When she got there, she
put the tooth proudly in its
place on the Fairy Queen's
new throne.

The next morning Holly read
her letter and smiled at her new
coin. She thought about the
Tooth Fairy and hoped that
she'd come again soon.

In fact … yes,
one of Holly's teeth
was definitely wobbly…

It was time to start
another letter to the
Tooth Fairy!

Also by Alan Durant

Other books by Vanessa Cabban.

Available from all good booksellers

www.walker.co.uk